MR.PERFECT

MR. PERFECT

by Roger Hargreaves

It was a perfect summer's day.

And on this perfect summer's day,
Mr Perfect was looking more perfect
than usual.

He didn't have a hair out of place

Mr Perfct lived in Tiptop Cottage.

And on this perfect summer's day,
his house was also looking even more
perfect than usual.

Not a curtain out of place.

I suppose you're wondering why
Tiptop Cottage was looking so perfect.

I shall tell you.

It was Mr Perfect's birthday,
and he was going to have a party.

There was a knock at the door.
"Perfect!" cried Mr Perfect.

"How very kind of you," he said, when he saw that all his guests had brought wonderful-looking presents.
"Please do come in, and if no one minds, we'll open the presents later."

Nobody minded in the least.

Well almost nobody.

"WHAT'S THAT?" roared Mr Uppity.

"I don't have any time to waste, you know!
You'd better make sure we
don't get bored today!"

Do you think this upset Mr Perfect?

Of course not.

Mr Perfect had perfect manners,
unlike rude Mr Uppity.

"Oh no, my dear Mr Uppity,
we shan't be bored today," he replied.
"First of all we shall dance."

And everybody danced.

Even Mr Uppity.

But although he danced, Mr Uppity
couldn't manage a smile.

Unfortunately, Mr Clumsy,
being his usual clumsy self,
broke a pile of plates.

Do you think this upset Mr Perfect?

Not at all.

"Don't worry, Mr Clumsy," said Mr Perfect.

And, being the perfect person he was,
and not in the least bit clumsy,
he produced a whole lot more plates ...

... made of cardboard!

Then, he brought in a cake.

It was huge.

It looked wonderful.

It smelt terrific.

And ...

Mr Greedy thought it tasted delicious.

He gobbled up the whole cake
in three seconds flat!

There wasn't a crumb left for anybody else!

Do you think this upset Mr Perfect?

Not in the least.

Being perfect, he had already guessed what would happen.

Quickly, he brought out lots of small cakes.

There were plenty for everybody.

Even Mr Perfect.

But as he was not greedy, he only ate one.

One cake was just perfect for him.

Once everything had been eaten,
Mr Perfect opened his presents.

He said as many thank-yous as
there were presents.

Well, not quite.

"What about my present?" cried Mr Mean.

Mr Mean's parcel was so small that
Mr Perfect had not seen it!

Mr Perfect opened the tiny parcel,
wrapped in newspaper.

"Oh, Mr Mean," said Mr Perfect.
"You've given me a lump of coal.
How kind of you!
It's delightful!"

"If I'd known, I'd only have given him
half a lump," grumbled Mr Mean.

"THAT'S IT! I've had enough!"
cried Mr Uppity, suddenly.

"I'm fed up with you, Mr Perfect. And do you
know why? I'll tell you! I have discovered
that there is a most enormous,unbearable,
exasperating fault with you."

"Would you be so kind as to tell me what
that might be?" asked Mr Perfect,
as politely as ever.

"Don't you understand?" cried Mr Uppity.
"Your fault is ...

... that you have NO faults!"

MR. MEN question time - can you help?
10 sets of 4 Mr. Men titles to be won!

Thank you for purchasing this Mr. Men book. We would be most grateful if you would help us with the answers to a few questions. Each questionnaire received will be placed in a monthly draw - you could win four Mr. Men books of your choice and a free bookmark! See overleaf.

Is this the first Mr. Men book you have purchased?   Yes ☐   No ☐   (please tick)

If No, how many books do you have in your collection?   ____

Have you collected any Little Miss books?   Yes ☐   No ☐   How many ____

Where do you usually shop for children's books?   Bookshop ☐   Supermarket ☐   Elsewhere ☐

(Can you name the retailer) _____

Which is your favourite Mr. Men character?   _____

Which is your favourite Little Miss character?   _____

Apart from Mr. Men/Little Miss which are your next two favourite children's characters?

1) _____   2) _____

Thank you for your help.
Return this form to: Marketing Department, Egmont Books Limited,
Unit 7, Millbank House, Riverside Park, Bollin Walk, Wilmslow, Cheshire SK9 1BJ.
Please tick overleaf which four Mr. Men books you would like to receive if you are successful in
our monthly draw and fill in your name and address details.

Signature of parent or guardian: _____   Age of Mr. Men fan: _____

We may occasionally wish to advise you of other children's books that we publish. If you would rather we didn't, please tick this box ☐

- ☐ 1. Mr. Tickle
- ☐ 2. Mr. Greedy
- ☐ 3. Mr. Happy
- ☐ 4. Mr. Nosey
- ☐ 5. Mr. Sneeze
- ☐ 6. Mr. Bump
- ☐ 7. Mr. Snow
- ☐ 8. Mr. Messy
- ☐ 9. Mr. Topsy-Turvy
- ☐ 10. Mr. Silly
- ☐ 11. Mr. Uppity
- ☐ 12. Mr. Small
- ☐ 13. Mr. Daydream
- ☐ 14. Mr. Forgetful
- ☐ 15. Mr. Jelly
- ☐ 16. Mr. Noisy
- ☐ 17. Mr. Lazy
- ☐ 18. Mr. Funny
- ☐ 19. Mr. Mean
- ☐ 20. Mr. Chatterbox
- ☐ 21. Mr. Fussy
- ☐ 22. Mr. Bounce
- ☐ 23. Mr. Muddle
- ☐ 24. Mr. Dizzy
- ☐ 25. Mr. Impossible
- ☐ 26. Mr. Strong
- ☐ 27. Mr. Grumpy
- ☐ 28. Mr. Clumsy
- ☐ 29. Mr. Quiet
- ☐ 30. Mr. Rush
- ☐ 31. Mr. Tall
- ☐ 32. Mr. Worry
- ☐ 33. Mr. Nonsense
- ☐ 34. Mr. Wrong
- ☐ 35. Mr. Skinny
- ☐ 36. Mr. Mischief
- ☐ 37. Mr. Clever
- ☐ 38. Mr. Busy
- ☐ 39. Mr. Slow
- ☐ 40. Mr. Brave
- ☐ 41. Mr. Grumble
- ☐ 42. Mr. Perfect
- ☐ 43. Mr. Cheerful
- ☐ 44. Mr. Cool
- ☐ 45. Mr. Rude
- ☐ 46. Mr. Good

Your name _____

Address _____

_____

_____ Postcode _____

3 Great Offers for MR.MEN Fans!

MR. MEN TOKEN

1 New Mr. Men or Little Miss Library Bus Presentation Cases

A brand new stronger, roomier school bus library box, with sturdy carrying handle and stay-closed fasteners.
The full colour, wipe-clean boxes make a great home for your full collection.
They're just £5.99 inc P&P and free bookmark!

☐ MR. MEN ☐ LITTLE MISS (please tick and order overleaf)

PLEASE STICK YOUR 50P COIN HERE

2 Door Hangers and Posters

In every Mr. Men and Little Miss book like this one, you will find a special token. Collect 6 tokens and we will send you a brilliant Mr. Men or Little Miss poster and a Mr. Men or Little Miss double sided full colour bedroom door hanger of your choice. Simply tick your choice in the list and tape a 50p coin for your two items to this page.

Door Hangers (please tick)
☐ Mr. Nosey & Mr. Muddle
☐ Mr. Slow & Mr. Busy
☐ Mr. Messy & Mr. Quiet
☐ Mr. Perfect & Mr. Forgetful
☐ Little Miss Fun & Little Miss Late
☐ Little Miss Helpful & Little Miss Tidy
☐ Little Miss Busy & Little Miss Brainy
☐ Little Miss Star & Little Miss Fun

Posters (please tick)
☐ MR.MEN
☐ LITTLE MISS

3 **Sixteen Beautiful Fridge Magnets –** **any 2 for £2.00!** inc.P&P

They're very special collector's items!
Simply tick your first and second* choices from the list below
of any 2 characters!

1st Choice

- [ ] Mr. Happy
- [ ] Mr. Lazy
- [ ] Mr. Topsy-Turvy
- [ ] Mr. Bounce
- [ ] Mr. Bump
- [ ] Mr. Small
- [ ] Mr. Snow
- [ ] Mr. Wrong

- [ ] Mr. Daydream
- [ ] Mr. Tickle
- [ ] Mr. Greedy
- [ ] Mr. Funny
- [ ] Little Miss Giggles
- [ ] Little Miss Splendid
- [ ] Little Miss Naughty
- [ ] Little Miss Sunshine

2nd Choice

- [ ] Mr. Happy
- [ ] Mr. Lazy
- [ ] Mr. Topsy-Turvy
- [ ] Mr. Bounce
- [ ] Mr. Bump
- [ ] Mr. Small
- [ ] Mr. Snow
- [ ] Mr. Wrong

- [ ] Mr. Daydream
- [ ] Mr. Tickle
- [ ] Mr. Greedy
- [ ] Mr. Funny
- [ ] Little Miss Giggles
- [ ] Little Miss Splendid
- [ ] Little Miss Naughty
- [ ] Little Miss Sunshine

*Only in case your first choice is out of stock.

--- **TO BE COMPLETED BY AN ADULT** ---

To apply for any of these great offers, ask an adult to complete the coupon below and send it with the appropriate payment and tokens, if needed, to MR. MEN OFFERS, PO BOX 7, MANCHESTER M19 2HD

- [ ] Please send _____ Mr. Men Library case(s) and/or _____ Little Miss Library case(s) at £5.99 each inc P&P
- [ ] Please send a poster and door hanger as selected overleaf. I enclose six tokens plus a 50p coin for P&P
- [ ] Please send me _____ pair(s) of Mr. Men/Little Miss fridge magnets, as selected above at £2.00 inc P&P

Fan's Name _____

Address _____

_____ **Postcode** _____

Date of Birth _____

Name of Parent/Guardian _____

Total amount enclosed £ _____

- [ ] **I enclose a cheque/postal order payable to Egmont Books Limited**
- [ ] **Please charge my MasterCard/Visa/Amex/Switch or Delta account** (delete as appropriate)

| | | | | | | | | | | | | | | | | | Card Number

Expiry date ___/___ **Signature** _____

Please allow 28 days for delivery. We reserve the right to change the terms of this offer at any time but we offer a 14 day money back guarantee. This does not affect your statutory rights.

MR.MEN **LITTLE MISS**
Mr. Men and Little Miss™ & ©Mrs. Roger Hargreaves

CUT ALONG DOTTED LINE AND RETURN THIS WHOLE PAGE